Maisy's Trick-or-Treat Sticker Book

Lucy Cousins

Take the sticker pages out of the middle of this book.
Open the pages so you can see the stickers
and the pictures in the book side by side.
Read the words on each page.
Then peel off a sticker and choose
where to put it in each picture.

CANDLEWICK PRESS

Today is Halloween!

Maisy and Cyril are painting faces on pumpkins.

It's fun to dress up for Halloween!

Dress Maisy as a sheriff and Panda as her deputy.

Look at Cyril's costume! Find Tallulah's fairy wand.

It's Eddie and Charley
playing a spooky trick!

Maisy loves to bob for apples. And so does Little Black Cat.

Now it's time to trick-or-treat.

Eek — what a scary house! Can you find the spiders?

Hooray! There's lots of candy for everyone.

Happy Halloween, Maisy!
Happy Halloween, everyone!